This is Moat Farm.

Zzzz.

Farmer Green lives on Moat Farm.

Ben and Neb
are sheepdogs.

Neb and Ben help on the farm.

This morning, Ben and Neb run up the hill...

...and help round
up the sheep.
Woof!

Farmer Green checks that the sheep are well.
Good sheep!

Neb and Ben rest in the back of the truck.